When CHRiSTMAS Came

WHEN CHRISTMAS Came

Written by Eileen Spinelli & Illustrated by Wayne Parmenter

ideals children's books.
Nashville, Tennessee

ISBN 0-8249-5507-2

Published by Ideals Children's Books
An imprint of Ideals Publications
535 Metroplex Drive, Suite 250
Nashville, Tennessee 37211
www.idealsbooks.com

Color separations by Precision Color Graphics, Franklin, Wisconsin

Printed and bound in Italy

Library of Congress Cataloging-in-Publication Data

Spinelli, Eileen.
  When Christmas came / written by Eileen Spinelli & illustrated by Wayne Parmenter.
    p. cm.
  Summary: As snow drifts higher and higher, the pastor of a small country church worries that no one will attend Christmas Eve services, but soon an unusual congregation gathers and shares the spirit of the season.
  ISBN 0-8249-5507-2 (alk. paper)
  [1. Christmas—Fiction. 2. Church—Fiction. 3. Clergy—Fiction. 4. Animals—Fiction.]
  I. Parmenter, Wayne, ill. II. Title.
  PZ7.S7566Wg 2005
  [E]—dc22
                        2005005154

Text previously published as *Coming Through the Blizzard*

10 9 8 7 6 5 4 3 2 1

Designed by Eve DeGrie

To the congregation of
The Presbyterian Church of Llanerch,
my beautiful church family. –E.S.

To my son Carson,
my little man with a big heart. –W.P.

One Christmas Eve
not long ago
it snowed.

And snowed.

And snowed.

Snow swirled against windows,
drifted deep against doors.

Snow buried cars and park benches.
Snow blanketed
the little brick church.

The minister shoveled the **wide** walkway.

He lit the candles.

He waited.

WHO would come through the night,
through the blizzard?
WHO would come to the Christmas Eve service?

The starling came

on snowy wings across a starless sky.
The starling came, frosty and fuddled,
to huddle on a cushion in candle glow,
beneath a branch of the shining tree.

The starling came.

The custodian came
on skis, earmuffed and bundled, trundling along—
CLIP-Clump, CLIP-Clump.

The custodian came,
chilly and true,
to dust the pews,
to stoke the furnace,
to place the star on top of the tree.

The custodian came.

Tom Cat came,

snarly and cold,
to slouch against the bubbling radiator,
then wrestle down a red ribbon
from the hanging greens.

Tom Cat came.

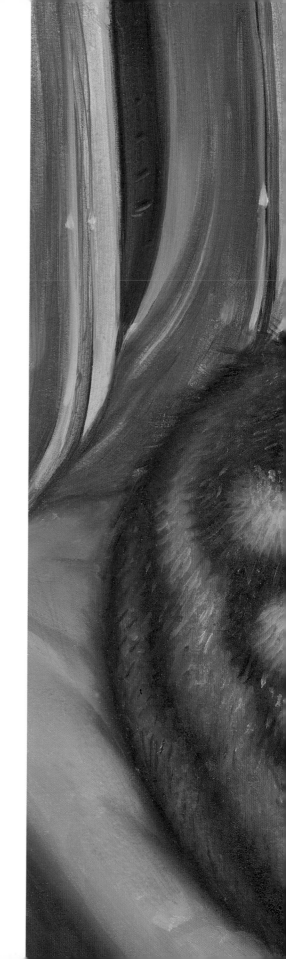

The small boy came,
trailing cookie crumbs,
quilted and cozy in his mother's arms.

The small boy came,

to drowse in

the sleepy scent of evergreen.

The small boy came.

Field mouse came

on tiny icicle toes
to nose for crumbs under the pew.
Field mouse came
skating across the organ keys
away from the cat.

Field mouse came.

The organist came,
breathless and brave,
with her backpack of music
and thermos of tea.

She brushed off the keys
and tested the pedals
and blew a breath of music
through the pipes.

The organist came.

Moth came,

silvery, silent,
blown from a pipe in the organ
on a burst of song,
a wordless HALLELUJAH.

Moth came.

The soloist came, red scarf round his neck, red-cheeked from the wind.

The soloist came,
to add the words,
to sing "GLORIA"
and "JOY TO THE WORLD."

The soloist came.

A stranger came,

midnight on her shoulders,

snow on her boots.

A stranger came,

alone

and shivering,

to peek past the door.

She saw the lights.

She felt the warmth.

She heard the carols.

A stranger came in.

A stranger came in.

Then . . .

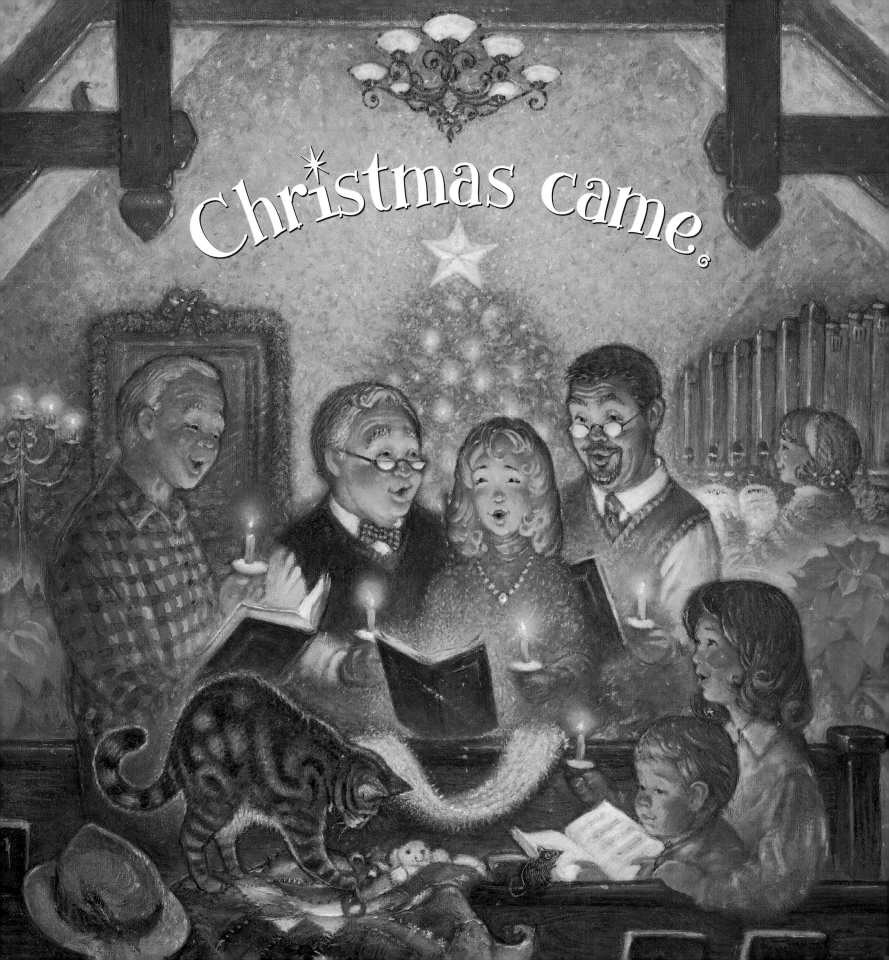

Christmas came.